FAMILIAR
STRANGER

FAMILIAR
STRANGER

A NOVEL

CAITLIN MOSS

For the people who love chocolate but hate Valentine's Day

one

NOW

"I want a divorce."

I freeze in the middle of steaming the dress I'm planning to wear tomorrow.

The words shock me.

Not because I didn't see the end coming—we've been racing full speed on a road that ends at a cliff, and I've been bracing myself for the fall for years. But now, hearing the four words I've been waiting to tumble out of his mouth makes me feel like I'm made of glass, and he just took a bat to my life.

"Did you hear me, Anna?"

I nod slowly, taking in each word with every dip of my chin.

He rubs his knees with his palms as he sits on the edge of

our bed, unsure of what to say next. "So…"

His voice trails off into our cold, dimly lit bedroom, and I finish the sentence for him. "I'll call the lawyer on Monday."

He nods, avoiding my eyes, as he throws on a hoodie. I tilt my head, studying my husband of ten years, feeling baffled. There's no yelling. No screaming. No throwing lamps or calling names. No passion. There aren't even tears. Those have all dried, leaving traces of salt on our skin we can't wash away no matter how hard we scrub.

He gets up to leave the room. He'll sleep on the couch again as usual. The kids don't notice because he's off to work before I even get them up for school.

My sweet babies. The only good thing to come out of this union.

I was always told that divorce is complicated and messy. I expected it to be loud and emotionally violent as it approached, but for us, it was a quiet cloud rolling over our sky.

When I was little, I squeezed my eyes shut and buried my head under a pillow when I heard my parents argue. I thought fighting meant a winner and a loser—an ending of a solid and sacred unit. Now I know that when the fighting stops, that's when you should really worry.

"John," I say.

He stills in the doorway and looks over his shoulder. "Let's not mention it this weekend, okay? I don't want my sister to suspect anything, and she needs to focus on the wedding. It's a happy time for my niece."

He pauses, chewing his bottom lip, then says, "Of course."

As he disappears in the dark hallway, I wonder how this could have all been prevented. I wonder what would have happened if I hadn't asked him to fall in love with me, if we hadn't fallen in love with an idea that, at the time, seemed perfect. It didn't seem permanent. And I guess, now, it would seem it still isn't. Because that's all love is. An idea. A feeling. A subjective emotion that morphs and changes over the years.

I run my fingers over the silk gown I'm wearing to my niece's wedding tomorrow. She's the first grandchild of the McKinley family to marry. She's young, fresh out of college, and full of dreams. She's done everything with a burning fire—a thirst that could never be quenched. A zest for life I used to know. Her mother and my oldest sister, Marie, used to joke that Serene is a carbon copy of me. I used to think that, too. But now I know differently.

I know how the world can steal from you. I know what it can take when you aren't looking. I know what it feels like to watch the burning fire turn to ashes.

I don't want that for my niece. I'll walk into the wedding tomorrow with hope for their future and hope that her new husband, Beau, will always remember how to love her, even when the world helps him forget.

And even though it's over and the love has run dry for me, I hope somewhere, deep down inside my husband's complacent heart, he remembers what it was like when we loved each other.

two

THEN

"Don't send it."

I held my breath as I heard the man's voice from behind me. It was warm and low, reminding me of how it felt to sit in front of a fire with a glass of red wine. I glanced at him as he moved to the barstool next to me. "I beg your pardon?" I asked.

"If you're thinking that hard before you send a text, you probably shouldn't," he said, sitting down. "Mind if I sit here?"

"You already are." I nodded at his seated position, and he smiled, amused. My gaze took in his dimples, and then I dragged my eyes up from my glass of white wine to meet the gaze of a man with the bluest eyes I had ever seen.

"Sorry. I was just—" I cut myself off. He didn't care what

I had been thinking about. "Just tired. Long week."

He nodded as he settled in and ordered a glass of cabernet sauvignon from the bartender.

"You'd think there's only one hotel in Seattle; it's so busy this weekend," he said as the bartender slid his glass on a cream-colored napkin.

"I don't mind crowds as long as everyone minds their own business." I shrugged.

He raised his eyebrows and let out a low breath of a laugh. "Well, all right then, I won't even be polite."

"Oh, I didn't mean—" though, maybe I did mean to be rude. I can't stand being hit on in a bar. I find it slimy no matter how expensive the drinks are or how many people are dressed in cocktail attire.

He threw up a hand and dipped his head. "No, I can take a hint. I will not even look at you. As a matter of fact, I'll just get up and find somewhere else to sit."

I grabbed his arm just as he raised his body from the seat. "Oh, stop."

He raised his eyebrows at my hand on his forearm, and the way his lips twitched to smile told me he was enjoying this.

"For one, the bar is packed. You won't find another seat. And two, I could use some company while I wait for my sister to pick me up."

He sat back down. "Well, since you begged."

I rolled my eyes, reeling in my smile.

"Another glass, ma'am?" the bartender asked.

"Sure."

"Sauvignon blanc?" he asked, and I nodded. "Did you have the Moreau or the Ricci?"

"Ricci."

"You should try the Moreau," the man beside me suggested.

I smiled politely, though I didn't care what he thought. "Why's that?"

"The type of grapes for sauvignon blanc grow best in the

Loire Valley in France, so it typically tastes better."

Pretentious ass.

"Hmm. I did not know that." Which was true. That, specifically, I did not know, though I was quite aware sauvignon is a French word. Naturally, the region where the wine originated is best.

"Just if you want a better glass of sauvignon blanc, you should probably choose the French wine over the Italian wine."

"What are you? A sommelier?"

He grinned. "Maybe in another life."

I nodded at him, slightly intrigued. "Well, I like Italian wine." The bartender paused, holding the bottle of wine in his hand. "The Ricci is fine. Thank you."

After the bartender filled my glass, I shifted to face the man next to me. He was wearing dark jeans and a gray t-shirt. He looked casual yet put together. Meanwhile, I was dressed in a black cocktail dress to wear to the rehearsal dinner of my little sister's funeral… I mean, wedding.

"You know, I couldn't help but notice you just ordered a Washington wine when everyone knows the grapes for a cabernet sauvignon also grow best in France," I comment.

His grin widened at this, his fingers dancing up and down the stem of his glass. "I like to support local."

I nodded, holding up my glass. "To each their own, I guess."

He raised his wine and clinked glasses with mine. The ring of the glass sang in the bar air like wedding bells, and we didn't break eye contact for a second.

"To each their own," he agreed.

My cheeks still were warm from my forward faux pas, but I made the most handsome man in the bar laugh, so I was calling it a win. I took another sip of my Italian wine.

"You here for the wedding or the graduation?" he asked. I glanced around the hotel bar. The University of Washington graduation was the following day, and so was the wedding. The lobby, bar, and restaurant were swarming with purple and gold tassels, cocktail attire, and out-of-town guests.

I tapped my phone with a wandering finger before answering, "Wedding."

Usually, I wouldn't have encouraged this kind of attention. But I didn't mind it tonight. I had always liked the idea of meeting someone in a city I didn't live in—even if my apartment was only an hour away. It would either be completely romantic, or I would end up on a true crime documentary, and both options sounded wildly exciting.

"Nice," he said, sipping his wine.

"You?" I asked, rotating my glass in my fingers.

"Oh, I'm not telling you. Stranger danger."

I laughed. "Oh, so mysterious. You're going to end up murdering me by the end of the night."

"Who said we're hanging out tonight?"

My cheeks warmed again, and I knew I was turning beet red this time. Stupid genetics never allowed me to hide my embarrassment.

His frown morphed into a smile, and my stomach flipped, making me shift on the bar seat. "I'm joking."

I smiled. "Me too."

He leans over. "And I'm here for the graduation."

"I figured," I said, sipping my wine.

"And why's that?"

I licked my lips. "Well, it's my little sister's wedding." I paused and looked at him. "I know just about everyone that will be there."

He nodded and smiled. "Fair."

"Who's graduating?" I asked.

"Little brother."

"Well, congratulations to him," I nodded, raising my glass. We clinked glasses, both making sure to maintain eye contact again. I smiled to myself. "I love graduations."

His brow twisted, and he drew back. "Who are you?"

"What? It's such a huge accomplishment and an incredible reason to celebrate."

"Excuse me…" he paused for dramatics, "Miss ma'am,

graduations are like one hundred hours long and boring enough to make even the most patient person want to stab their eyes out."

I laughed, shifting closer with a slight shrug of my shoulders. "I'd rather go to the graduation tomorrow."

He shook his head. "You'd rather go to my little brother's five-hour graduation than your little sister's wedding?"

"Yes." I took a long drink.

"I don't believe you," he said with a breath of a laugh.

"Well," I begin, resting my glass on the bar top. "You might if you realized I am smack dab in the middle of three daughters, born to Augustus and Ellen McKinley, named the most simple names to balance out our great expectations—Marie, Anna, Jenn. My oldest sister, Marie, is a doctor who managed to get through medical school as a single mom. She met her doctor-husband while there and has lived happily ever after since. And my youngest sister, Jenn, also a doctor, will be marrying the boy next door we knew growing up that magically became a lawyer—because, of course, he did."

"So because they have successful jobs, you don't want to celebrate them?" he asked.

I scoffed at his devil's advocacy. "No," I emphasized. "I want to go to the wedding. I would just *rather* go to a college graduation of some stranger's little brother. Not because I'm heartless or a bitch, but because I'm tired of being compared to my siblings. Marie had her MD. by this age. Jenn had a ring on her finger by her first year of residency. She got a 4.0. She made the dean's list. She's top of the program. She was matched with the most sought-after residency." I listed each accomplishment off in a snarky tone, and as soon as I tasted my own bitterness in my words, I let out a breath. "They are successful and happy and managed to become doctors like Dad always wanted, and meanwhile, I am just Anna, the certified black sheep of the family. Medical school drop-out with a broken engagement who works at a bookstore in Gig Harbor."

A quiet settled between us, and I knew he was absorbing

my rant. "Well, you are a bright, shining red flag, aren't you?"

I laughed. I knew he was teasing. "Better run now."

"Are you trying to seduce me?" His smile indicated I was, and it was working.

"No, just torture you."

He laughed. "Listen, sibling dynamics are tough," he said, and I nodded. "But doing your own thing isn't a bad thing. Not everyone's life follows the same formula. Finding what we want out of life is not always a this-then-that scenario. Sometimes, it's a lot of rejection, mistakes, and years until we figure it all out."

I stared at him, my chin resting in my hand. "Tell that to my sisters."

"Ah, fuck 'em." He waved a hand in the air and took another sip of his wine. I always loved a man drinking wine. The delicate glass in his large hands, taking small sips, knowing he could swallow it in one gulp if he wanted. It's the swirl. The smell. It's the care and restraint that makes drinking wine so sexy.

"I'm going to tell my mom you said that." A coy smile spread over my lips.

"I hope you do." He leaned closer, and his scent hit me, sending a chill down my spine and settling deep in my gut. I didn't know if it was the wine or the conversation, but I suddenly found myself very attracted to him. I took him in for a moment—bright blue eyes. Sharp jaw, softened by dimples and the perfect amount of scruff speckled along his face. His hair was dark—almost black—and his outfit was casual, and yet he was still so striking. It had only been minutes, but it seemed like time didn't matter.

"Want to know a secret?" I asked, breaking the silence and drumming my fingers along the bar top.

"No," he deadpanned, and my mouth dropped as my head snapped in his direction. "I'm a teacher, which makes me a mandatory reporter."

"You're a teacher? What grade?"

"Tenth grade English."

"That sounds terrible," I remarked, wanting to swallow my tongue, but he laughed. "Sorry."

"It's not so bad, but being a mandatory reporter is quite difficult when I am a devoted believer in minding your business."

I threw back my head and laughed. "Well, it's not that kind of secret. Relax."

He rubbed his brow and said, "Phew. In that case, yes. Tell me all your secrets."

He licked his lip as he said this, distracting me from what I would tell him. When his teeth caught the side of his lip, I remembered.

"I kissed the groom once," I confessed.

He gasped, but I could tell he was exaggerating, so I smacked his shoulder. "Come on! Don't make fun of me. That's weird, right? My sister is marrying him."

He laughed. "Well, when did you kiss him?"

"Eighth grade. After we played spin the bottle." I sipped my wine.

"No one plays spin the bottle in real life," he scoffed.

"Well, not now at twenty-eight, but once upon a time, we played," I argued. "We were actually done with the game, and he whispered in my ear, I wish the bottle landed on you. Then he pulled me into the hall closet and kissed me."

He shrugged and then leaned in like my secret was far more salacious. "Did you slip him some tongue?"

I shook my head, meeting his eyes. "No, but he did."

"Uh-oh, I'm going to have to tell your sister." He pulled out his phone. "What's her name? I'm sure I can find her on Instagram."

I held his hand and pushed it back down on the bar. "Oh! You are a snitch!"

He cocked an eyebrow. "Mandatory reporter."

I snorted out a laugh and shook my head. "Is that the politically correct term for snitch?"

"Yes," he answered.

I shook my head, biting my lip hard enough I couldn't

physically smile. "You're something else."

"So are you."

When he smiled at me, my knotted stomach was now doing cartwheels.

"So, is that who you were thinking of texting earlier?" he asked. "Trying to confess before she walks down the aisle to her death... er, I mean, happily ever after."

I loved that he was playing into my blatant pessimism. I let out a breath of a laugh, looking at my hands in thought. "No, I was going to invite an old friend to the wedding, so I'm not dateless."

He nodded. "But you hesitated because you don't want to see him again, do you?"

My lips twitched to smile, but I did my best to not give myself away. "It's just hard to be single at a wedding when everyone knows what happened two years ago. I mean, half of the guests received my Save the Date followed by an email that said 'we regret to inform you' four months later..." I swallowed my humiliation. I wasn't angry we weren't getting married. I was embarrassed. I said yes to someone I didn't want to spend the rest of my life with. "Anyway, this guy I knew in college lives around here, and I almost asked him to protect me from the monsters haunting me for my past choices." I turned away, realizing how much information I was revealing to someone I just met.

"So, who do you want to make jealous tomorrow?"

I raised my eyebrows. "I'm sorry?"

"Tomorrow," he said. "Do you want to make your sisters jealous or the groom?"

I rolled my eyes with a helpless smile. "I don't want to make anyone jealous. I don't want the comparison. For one day, I want to celebrate my sisters without hearing the pity from everyone that I'm still single and way less successful."

"What time is the wedding?"

"Seven," I answered with a hint of uncertainty.

"Tell you what. My brother's graduation should be over by four. I will go to the wedding with you."

I jerked back. "I don't…" My voice fell silent. The rational part of my brain did not think this was a good idea. But I wasn't known for being rational. I was known for dropping out of medical school and calling off weddings. Swimming upstream was my favorite sport. Letting go and doing the unthinkable was very on-brand for me. "Are you sure? I'm a walking red flag."

He shrugged. "Red is my favorite color."

I cocked an eyebrow. "You really are going to kill me, aren't you?"

He smiled a wickedly charming smile. "Only if you torture me first."

three

NOW

"I'm going to go clean the grill," John says as I unclamp the curling iron, letting a long, brunette ringlet go.

"Why?" I ask, grabbing another strand of hair to curl.

"Because it's dirty." He shrugs.

"It's February. You won't be grilling until May at the earliest, and by then—" I cut myself off, letting go of another ringlet. "You know what, don't worry about it. Do what you feel is necessary."

What he is choosing to do is in no way necessary, but *go right fucking ahead, John.*

He nods once with an irritated jilt of his chin as if I'm the one causing the tension because it couldn't possibly be that I still need to curl Suzy's hair, iron Henry's suit, pack extra snacks for the ceremony in case they get bored, and feed them lunch before we leave because the reception isn't even set to begin until six and we have to be at the church at two for pictures. Not to mention, I myself need to get ready for my niece's wedding.

There have been instances in the past when I would have expressed my irritation, rattling off a to-do list in hopes that John would automatically delegate some tasks to himself. Instead, he always stared at me doe-eyed like none of it was his problem while I continued to carry the mental load. It reached the point where it was much easier to assume he would take care of nothing. Worrying whether or not he'd like to contribute to our family practically turned out to be another item taking up headspace, and I no longer have the bandwidth for it.

Suzy pops into the bathroom as I finish my hair. "Mommy, can I wear makeup like you?"

I smile at her. "Maybe not like me, but a little, okay?"

"Okay, can I put my dress on now?" she asks, skipping across the tiled floors.

"Let's eat lunch first," I answer, tightening my robe and ushering her out of my bathroom and downstairs.

As I finish making instant macaroni and cheese paired with steamed broccoli and sliced apples, I holler for Henry in the playroom to join us. He reluctantly pulls away from his toys, and they both devour their lunches. The amount of artificial cheese on each of their chins and shirts makes me give a subconscious pat on my back for not having them get dressed yet.

"Where's Daddy?" Henry asks, taking a long slurp of water.

"Outside," I say, then add inside my head, *cleaning the grill because he'd rather do that than participate in this family.*

"He's coming to Serene's wedding, right?" Suzy asks, smacking her broccoli.

"Close your mouth when you chew, please," I chide softly. "And yes, of course, he's coming."

She shrugs, satisfied with the answer.

I check the time. We need to leave in forty-five minutes. "Okay, finish up, please. I still have to do your hair and iron your suit, Henry."

Their heads bob in acknowledgment, and I hurry upstairs to iron Henry's suit, only burning my hand once. I lay his suit on my bed and call for Suzy to come upstairs to do her hair, but I forgot to plug the curling iron back in.

"Dammit," I mutter, feeling the deadline to leave inching closer.

"What's that mean?" she asks.

"Oh, nothing… darn it," I correct my language and hoist her up on the counter. "Shall we do your makeup?"

She squeals and claps her hands together. I don't add much—she's only seven. But a little blush on her cheeks and highlighter on her lids goes a long way. I open my makeup drawer to her and help her off the counter. "Pick out your lipstick."

"Any color?" she asks, eyes wide in amazement.

I smirk at her. "Within reason."

She pulls out all twelve tubes, lining them up based on color. Pinks, mauves, corals, reds. Shimmery, glossy, matte. She's an expert organizer when pressed to make a decision.

I let her take her time while I curl her hair.

"Mom, can you help me?!" Henry yells from the other room.

"If you need me, come get me!" I holler back, not unkindly.

I hear his footsteps stomp through the upstairs until he reaches the bathroom. "Mom, can you help me?"

I raise my eyebrows.

"Please," he adds. Manners are brutal at five.

"Not right this second. If it's important, you can ask Dad."

"I did. He said to ask you."

My jaw tightens. *Of course, he did.* "Well, what do you need help with?"

"Opening my toothpaste."

A brief wave of gratefulness passes through me at the simplicity of the task. "Sure, bring it here."

Once the toothpaste is opened, John enters the bathroom in a T-shirt and jeans. "I need to shower."

"We're almost done," I answer, not meeting his eye.

He huffs slightly, and I don't roll my eyes because I don't care about his inconveniences. I clip back our daughter's hair and overspray her with hairspray. Then, order them to both get their fancy outfits on.

Henry needs help with his tie.

Suzy needs help tying the back of her dress.

They're picture-perfect. I sit them in front of the television and make them promise not to move until I return from getting dressed.

"Mom, my lipstick," Suzy reminds me, holding up the tube she selected in her palm.

"Oh, right. We'll do it at the church, okay?"

I rush upstairs to put on my dress and add my jewelry. John is escaping the shower. I don't look, nor do I feel weird that my almost ex-husband's penis is swinging around in the same room as me. I've seen it for over ten years, and the dynamic we've created with each other has made our naked bodies very uninteresting.

"You aren't ready yet?"

My gaze snaps to his. "No, too busy getting everyone else ready."

"They're old enough to get ready by themselves, though, aren't they?" he asks, throwing on his boxer briefs and suit pants.

I almost laugh at how he phrases the question as if he doesn't know what his kids are capable of.

"It's a wedding, John," I reason.

He shrugs, holding up two ties. "Which tie?"

"Burgundy. It's a Valentine's Day wedding," I answer.

There's a flash of pain and remorse that scurries over his expression. "Right. Happy Valentine's Day."

"Happy Valentine's Day."

Neither of us is emotional or upset as we say the words. We always thought it was a stupid holiday, despite my love affair with chocolate. I thought it was preposterous that anyone should need a reminder to give the love of their life flowers. And John always hated the taste of the chocolates inside the cardboard hearts.

But my niece insisted on a Valentine's Day Wedding. I'm sure it will be lovely. And I hope her marriage is even better.

"I'll go load up the kids," John says, shrugging on his jacket.

"I'll be right down."

Life together has always been this awkward song and dance with no rhythm or passion for years. We've been walking in this routine of complacency for so long that we rarely misstep. But every time we're forced to perform one more time, it becomes more and more abundantly clear that it's time to find our own dance.

four

THEN

I laughed when he offered to be my date at my sister's wedding, but his expression told me he wasn't joking. "Oh, you're really serious. You want to go to my sister's wedding."

"I mean, I already know where it is." There was mischief in his smile as he turned in the chair to face me square on. He wasn't touching me, not even reaching, yet I still felt so consumed by him. I was certain he could swallow me whole if he did actually put his hands on me. I shifted on my chair, squeezing my knees together.

"You understand what that means, right?"

He just stared, eyes hooded, a knowing expression written all over his features.

"Like meeting my family…" I continued, dragging out the last word with trepidation.

His mouth dropped in dramatic shock as he held a hand to his chest. "Oh, you mean your family will be at your sister's wedding? In that case, absolutely not."

I laughed at his sarcasm, swatting his knee. "What does this entail? Like, are you an escort? Are you expecting me to pay you in cash… or…" My voice trailed off. I was entirely unsure of how transactions like this go.

He laughed, diffusing my nerves. "I am not an escort. You don't have to pay me. I'm doing it to be nice. You seem fun. I love a celebration."

I narrowed my eyes. "Unless it's a graduation."

"Exactly." He punctuated the word by pointing at me. "See? An hour into getting to know each other, we are already in sync. This is going to be the perfect match."

I laughed at the sentiment. "Are we crazy?"

"Of course, we're crazy. But it'll be fun."

"I just met you. This won't even be believable. My sisters will see right through this."

He paused, eyes examining me, turning my barstool toward him and pulling me closer. The movement was fast and smooth; the stool barely made a sound against the floor. My breath caught at his close proximity, and I did my best to subdue my breathing. His legs encased mine as he ran his fingertips up my thigh to just below the hem of my dress. I squeezed my legs tighter together, holding my breath as he whispered against my ear, "I will make certain every guest there believes you are well taken care of." His breath trailed against my neck, and goosebumps rose on my flesh.

I was ridiculously flustered. It was an act; I had known him for barely an hour, yet I was so into it. I forced myself to pull back, sinking my teeth into my bottom lip. "You're rather good at this. Are you sure you aren't an escort?"

He laughed, his face erupting with boyish charm yet strong, unmistakable confidence.

"Fine. Let's do it," I conceded. "But under one condition."

"What's that?"

"We have to use a fake name for you."

He flashed me a curious smile.

"Just in case someone tries to google you or look you up on social media. Because my sisters will do that."

His adorably smug eyebrows twisted. "At a wedding?"

"Yes!" I answered so enthusiastically that he reared his square chin back and smirked.

"Deal. What's my name?"

I twisted my lips as I studied him. Good question. I had spent the last hour sizing him up, letting the lust rush through my veins, but naming him never crossed my mind.

"Mark."

"No," he deadpanned.

My jaw dropped. "What? Why?"

"Let's be a little interesting."

"Mark is a classic. Mark is reliable. Mark is who you call for a favor."

"Mark is forgettable." He raised his eyebrows, and I knew instantly he wasn't wrong.

"Okay, fine. I got it." I paused for effect as I examined him. He didn't look like a Mark. I knew exactly what he looked like. "Isaac."

A slow smile spread over his lips as he nodded. "Last name?"

"Morrison," I answered immediately. "Profession?"

"Teacher. It'll be easier if we keep it as close to the truth."

"Good point," I agreed. "How did we meet?"

He shrugged. "At a bar."

I deflated a bit and gave him a look.

He restrained a smile, then said, "Fine. I order books from the bookstore you work at for my classroom. One day, I brought you coffee, and you laughed because you didn't realize I knew your coffee order. But you always had it sitting on top of the counter. Grande vanilla americano, no cream. You were impressed I got it right. I was just impressed by you. Then one day, and many Americanos later, I asked you out."

I smiled at this telling of our non-meeting. "What did we do?"

"We took out a Seattle Donut Boat in the Puget Sound, but you're a terrible driver and ran into a large piece of driftwood, and it got caught in the engine—"

"That wouldn't happen—"

"You sure?" He raised his eyebrows with a smile buried in his lips.

"Fine. It happened," I answered, thoroughly entranced in playing make-believe with this familiar stranger.

"Right, and even though we were stranded for an extra hour and had to pay a maintenance fee, neither of us cared because we had actual donuts on board." In one swift gesture, he swept my long brown hair over my shoulder, cradling my neck in his hand, "And we had each other."

My breath hitched in my throat. It all felt so magical so quickly.

"Did we kiss?" I asked with a breath.

"Of course, and it tasted like chocolate frosting," he said, his voice low and raspy in the dimly lit bar.

The blood was rushing through my ears, and my stomach felt tight with need, but I managed to say, "I like that first date."

His lips moved even closer to mine as he whispered, "So will your sisters."

I let out a low laugh as he brushed a strand of hair from my face, and I whispered, "I'm not going to take you up to my room."

His smile grew. "And so the torture begins."

I laughed as our faces stayed breaths apart, his hand on my cheek, the other wrapped around my waist.

"But also," he added. "That's presumptuous. I haven't even tried to kiss you."

"But you should, right?" I teased. "I mean, we should practice. If we kiss for the first time in front of two hundred people I know in real life, and it's awkward, this will all be for nothing—"

He didn't wait for me to complete my sentence. His strong hand gently found my neck and tilted my mouth to his by the jaw. For such an abrupt movement, his lips still landed on mine softly. I could taste the wine on his lips and smell the aftershave on his skin. My eyes fell closed, and I drifted into a dreamlike state of mind that simultaneously felt like I was drowning downstream and floating on a cloud. With the gentle pressure of his hand on my neck and the other on my hip, he woke up all my senses.

I didn't think it could feel like that so soon. I had kissed a stranger before, but never a stranger that kissed me like they had known me my whole life. They call it falling, but that kiss felt like dancing. It felt like a kiss I had waited for my entire life. His hands cradled my body like he already knew it, and his mouth moved against mine with soft yet skilled movements. I wanted more. It was like a needle that found a vein. A drug that found a feen. A person that found their person.

I pressed a reluctant hand on his chest and pulled back, licking the taste of him off my lips.

"Well, if this is your idea of torture…" he teased with a smile.

I breathed out a laugh as my gaze snapped to my buzzing phone. It was lit up with a text from my older sister, Marie.

I frowned when I read it. "I have to go. My sister is outside to pick me up for the rehearsal dinner. I'm sorry. Can I get your number, and I'll text you the details about tomorrow?"

He took my phone from me as I held it out to him. "Sure. And I can't make it to the rehearsal tonight because I had to do a last-minute parent-teacher conference before school is out next week."

He finished typing his number into my phone and handed it back to me. "Right. And we both live in…" I waited for his answer, hoping he remembered where I was from.

"Gig Harbor."

"Good job." I smiled, needing to pull back and walk away

but not wanting to. "See you tomorrow, *Isaac*. Don't bail on me."

He took my hand in his and kissed it, leaving tingles on my skin. "I would never."

As I walked out of the hotel to meet my sister with her husband and daughter, Serene, I opened my phone to see he saved his number as Isaac Morrison. Then I realized he texted himself: *the most beautiful girl you've ever met. Save this number immediately.*

My chest fluttered with giddy nerves. It was a stupid prank to pull on my sister's wedding day. But I didn't care.

"Why are you smiling like that?" Marie asked as I slid into the backseat and booped eleven-year-old Serene on the nose.

"I'm just excited for tomorrow."

five

NOW

"You look nice," John says, adjusting his tie. I glance at him in the mirror.

"Thank you. You do, too." I don't say more, and I'm not sure I should. He looks more than nice. He always does. He aged unimaginably well. All hints of his boyish charm evaporated when he hit thirty-two. All the soft lines of his face sharpened, and his facial hair is peppered with gray. The broadness of his shoulder is more rugged. His entire presence is all around more pronounced, as if his energy has no problem taking up space. I don't find myself angry when I look at him. Not even sad. I am simply curious. I don't know him anymore. And he doesn't know me.

We forgot years ago after we stopped asking. We stopped caring.

I fasten the back of my second earring, smooth out the maroon silk of my dress, and admire my figure. My hips are curvier than they used to be, and the smile lines around my mouth are also more pronounced. But at forty, I am more confident than I've ever been.

"The kids are in the car," he comments, adjusting his cufflink.

I glance at the clock—we're barely on time.

I finish putting on my lipstick and nod. As we exit the bedroom, he rests a hand on my lower back, guiding me through the house. *Our* house, though it doesn't feel like either of us has ownership in it anymore.

The once-bright walls seem cold and unapologetic. The smiling faces in the picture frames hanging on the wall seem inauthentic and staged. I've been walking around this house with this man for ten years, and I still feel like a stranger in my own life.

"Buckle up, sweeties," I say to our kids in the back seat.

John clears his throat as we pull out of the driveway, and my eyes stay glued on the house's exterior, wondering who will live in it next. I wonder if they'll find the happy ending I thought I would have. Or I wonder if they'll lose each other inside the walls just like we did.

We drive in silence while the kids sing along to the latest Kidz Bop until we reach the old church downtown. It's white with a bright red door. It always struck me as a church from a horror film, where they must have conjured demons from the leader of the Bible study after she confessed to cheating on her husband. It spooked me in a way that drew me to it. Maybe I should've taken that as a sign not to get married there. Perhaps if I had listened to my gut on my wedding day when I chose to marry the stable man next to me, we wouldn't be arriving at this same church, the front concrete steps still wet with February's morning dew, putting on fake smiles and wishing my sweet niece congratulations for her happy marriage when our own is crumbling to pieces.

"Have you talked to Serene?" John asks as we sit in a pew

on the bride's side.

I smile. "Not today, but she seemed so excited yesterday at the rehearsal."

He nods, then says in a low voice, "I'm sorry I missed it."

I nod, but I know he's not sorry. Missing things has become his entire existence. Graduations. Birthdays. Promotions. Dinner reservations. Each RSVP he regretfully declined was always met with a solid excuse that left me lonely and hopeless.

I've purchased many beautiful dresses to wear to date nights I never attended. Many still hang, sad and dusty, with the tags on in my closet.

Once upon a time, he loved a celebration. But that was then, back when he loved me.

six

THEN

I stared at the leaf design in the form of my latte, tapping the glass of the coffee cup with itching fingers as I stared at the black mirror of my phone. I wound up regretfully drinking two more glasses of wine at the rehearsal dinner and drunk-texted "Isaac Morrison" a mirror selfie in the bathroom.

This is all yours tomorrow! I had texted with a popped hip, kissy face, and peace sign against the burgundy floral wallpaper.

Gag.

That fourth glass of wine and the memory of him whispering in my ear had me feeling Sexy with a capital S. By the following day, loaded with 400 milligrams of ibuprofen, twenty ounces of water, and three shots of espresso, I was quite embarrassed and confident he regretted agreeing with the drunk bimbo in the hotel bar that still throws up peace signs in pictures.

Reluctantly, I swiped the phone off the table to text him and tell him to forget about what we agreed to, only to find a reply from him.

I shut my eyes and took a deep breath, steeling myself for some well-deserved rejection.

Instead, I found myself blushing at his own mirror selfie—clearly taken in his hotel room—mimicking my pose and a text that read, *I can't wait.* Only in his, he wasn't wearing a cute cocktail dress but was shirtless and wearing black sweatpants with just the band of his underwear sticking out. My heart started pounding, and this warm wave rushed through my belly.

His hair was still messy with sleep, and a tattoo was scrawled across his ribcage, but I couldn't make out what it said. He was ripped and adorable. My jaw was slack as I examined every pixel of the selfie sent to me, but I still jumped when another text rolled in.

Sorry, I didn't respond last night. I was sleeping.

I bit my lip and smiled at my phone like a ridiculous cheeseball.

I wish I had done that last night, too

I shot out the text and panicked, wishing an unsend button existed.

I mean, not with you.

Just sleeping

And not drinking wine.

Though I'm sure you're a fine person to sleep next to, I just didn't want you to think I was objectifying you.

Or anything.

I rattled each embarrassing text off so fast that I couldn't figure out how to backtrack.

Sorry. I'm a lot better in person.

A few seconds later, he texted back.

I know, but you're also cute when you panic.

God, he was so damn sweet. It made my chest hurt.

Where are you right now? I'm headed down to the hotel restaurant for breakfast. Are you hungry?

I licked my lips and hesitated.

I'm already down here. Finishing up...

I hit send, feeling slightly disappointed.

Don't leave yet. I'll be down in five.

Nerves churned in my gut but so did something else. It rang through my senses as excitement, and I knew it was because of the mystery of it all. We were writing the story of us moment by moment, creating an untouchable love story because it wasn't real.

"Hey, you," his voice rumbled over my skin, and he pressed his minty mouth to my cheek to kiss it.

I startled, but only slightly, before I leaned in. "Hey," I say back.

He sat down across the white marble table. "You look beautiful." It was such a simple compliment, but the richness of his tone and the way his gaze traveled over my face with a smile made it feel like he's only ever said those words to me.

I smiled slowly, letting the expression of happiness fill my face until it reached my eyes... and I felt the crinkle of the gold patches under my eyes.

"Oh my God!" I shrieked, pinching the patches off my face and tossing them to the table with a well-lubricated splat. "I didn't know I still had those on!" I slapped my hands over my eyes and groaned.

Isaac let out a low chuckle and leaned closer. "You were rocking those eye patches. I was impressed," he teased.

"I ate an entire omelet while wearing those... in public!" I whisper-yelled.

"Everybody wears those. Don't freak out."

"This is a nice hotel."

"The waiter probably didn't even notice."

"The waiter probably told everyone in the back that the poor hungover girl forgot to take her eye patches off and looks like a washed-up suburban housewife whose husband just left her," I countered.

"That's aggressive. Calm down."

"Why didn't you say anything when you walked in?"

He shrugged. "Because I don't care if you have gold eye patches on or a brown paper bag. You're beautiful."

I let out a deep breath. "You're very good at not breaking character. Are you sure you're not a professional actor?"

"Who said I'm acting?" he asked, locking his blue eyes on me.

A sheath of vulnerability spread over every inch of my skin.

"Can I get you anything?" the server said, directing her question to Isaac.

He cleared his throat. "Could I get the All-American with

pancakes and sausage?"

The server nodded and then disappeared. Isaac inched closer. He had this way about him, slowly consuming my space in gestures and in words. He also had this way about him that made me want him to consume more than just my space and my time. I had only known him eighteen hours, but it felt like eighteen years.

He tucked my hair behind my ear and whispered, "I don't want you to take this the wrong way, but you need to pretend like you like me."

"I think you're misunderstanding why my guard is up."

A sly, mischievous grin danced across his face, and he looked far less like a high school teacher and reminded me more of a villain from the books I love that you're supposed to hate but don't.

His smile dipped with his gaze and then returned to me. "I appreciate that, but what I meant was, I'm fairly certain the women at the table to your seven o'clock know you, and they're wondering all about me."

My eyes widened. Of course, someone who knew me… or my sister at the very least would be at breakfast. The hotel offered a special rate for her wedding guests.

"Relax," he whispered, running his fingers under my jaw and tilting my chin toward his face. I held my breath, waiting for him to kiss me. "You're mine today, remember?"

I restrained a smile. I couldn't understand how this wildly attractive man could send me a goofball text and command my entire presence with one word I usually hate to hear. Because, let's be honest, being told to relax typically has the opposite effect.

Then he kissed me.

I kept my eyes open like a weirdo because I was nervous, and my attempt to relax failed miserably.

He laughed. "Come on, Anna, you look like a deer in headlights."

I shook my head. "Right, right. No, I got this. I can kiss you. I can pretend. I can—" I didn't finish my sentence because I went in for a kiss too aggressively. It was not the same kiss as the previous night. This one more or less was like head-butting him with my mouth.

He drew back, cradling his face. "Did you bite me?"

I winced. "Sorry. I got excited."

He let out another low laugh and wet his lips. "Where's the girl I met last night?"

"The girl you met last night is terrified we won't pull this off, and I will become an even bigger joke than I am."

The honesty felt good to admit, but I was also sure it made me even more pathetic.

He sat back as the server arrived with his meal, and my phone vibrated loudly on the table. Marie's name lit up the screen.

"Oh shit," I muttered. "I need to go upstairs and get my hair and makeup done. I'm five minutes late."

"Do what you must do," he said, standing as I did. He grabbed my hand. "Tell me if you don't want to do this, and I won't show up."

"No, I want to." I hesitated for a half second, then added. "I think it will be more fun with you."

seven

NOW

I jump as John takes my hand, lacing our fingers together while we sit in the pew. He notices my discomfort, squeezes twice, and then lets my hand go.

I should want him to hold my hand if only to make everything seem perfectly fine. And deep down, I want to remember when it was. When he held my face and kissed my lips. When it was all new and exciting and unknown. He didn't know me, and I didn't know him. Every moment was an unveiling until we had finally stripped down every layer of each other, reaching the other's core and discovering we no longer liked what we saw.

We still played the part fine for family pictures. Even though we won't be married much longer, I'm content to have him a part of this day. He met Serene when she was so young. She loved him—she still does. Sometimes marriages sever, but family is still family.

I shoot a side glance at John, wondering what events like this will look like in the future and if I'm being overly optimistic in thinking he'll stick around for anything related to my side of the family.

I exhale tomorrow's worries and focus on the wedding before me.

Beau stares down at Serene with tears in his eyes while the pastor speaks. She turns to her maid of honor, Kiley, for extra tissue, and as she spins back around, the train of her gown twists, and Kiley steps forward to straighten it out for the photographer. The shutter of the camera reminds me how picturesque this moment is. How, just ten years ago, I was the bride in the picture. I had the long train, and my hair curled in long waves down my back. John had tears in his eyes and a perfectly tailored suit, just like Beau.

We had the guests. The music. The rings. The pastor. And the promises.

But we couldn't keep it—neither of us.

"We don't get to choose who we fall in love with," the pastor says, "but I promise you, the act of love is a choice. Every day. For better or for worse." He pauses for effect, then adds, "Just ask my wife."

The guests chuckle, and John lets out a breath of a laugh that really sounds like, hmmph. I don't laugh. I wince because I hate this brand of pastoral humor.

I glance up at John and accidentally make eye contact. We stay there a moment, both our gazes asking, remember when?

Remember when it was you and I promising forever? When we thought for better or for worse, it meant beach vacations and forgetting to put the toilet seat down. We didn't know the uphill battles we would face in the years to come. A part of my brain wishes we could return to when it was new and I didn't know what he could do. When I didn't know we could destroy each other slowly. We didn't mean to hurt each other, of course not. But we pricked at wounds we didn't know existed, and then gradually, year after year, we bled out until there was nothing left.

I blink my gaze away from his first. It's always me first. When he goes in for a kiss. When he asks for a hug. When he wants to know how my day is, I pull away. I shrug. I give short answers and sigh too loudly. It's always me first.

I remember telling him I didn't want this life. I didn't like the routine. The boring dinners at six o'clock sharp. The perfectly manicured lawn. The reasonably sized SUV and the sedan. The turning over without a kiss goodnight. I didn't sign up for any of it. He cried and said, "Yes, you did! We may not have known what it would look like when we made the vow, but you promised a life with me, Anna; you did!"

He was right. I promised him a life.

But he promised to love me.

We both failed.

The ceremony saunters on with the cadence of most weddings. The pastor ends with something thoughtful. Beau and Serene exchange vows that make us laugh and cry. They say I do. Beau kisses her with just the right amount of passion, even though we know they're probably yearning for more. As Serene takes her bouquet from her maid of honor and stands next to Beau, the photographer's camera shutters a few more times, flash freezing their smiles in time to hang on their walls for years to come.

As she passes by with her new husband, I toss the rose petals in the aisle. She makes eye contact with me, and her smile widens. I can hear her voice squealing, "Auntie A, I'm married!" in my mind.

I smile back, wide and as hopeful as I can, but tears are in my eyes because I can't help but wonder what hardship they will face. What trial they must endure. I wonder what will try to break them.

Because every marriage breaks at some point, and they can't always get put back together.

eight

THEN

"Oh! And I have someone I want you to meet tonight!" Jenn shimmied in her corseted gown while Marie finished fastening the silk buttons.

"Oh please, you know Anna doesn't care about meeting anybody after what happened with Seth," Marie said, fluffing the back of Jenn's dress.

I blotted my lips and shot her a sharp glare. "Let's not talk about that."

"We aren't going to talk about it, Anna Banana," Marie chastised with a condescending tone. "But Jenn and I both know you are not ready to date since he ripped your life apart."

"*I* was the one who called it off!"

Jenn and Marie turned to me in unison, hands on their

hips with identical expressions of accusations.

"What? I'm fine!" But the whiny tone in my voice made me sound bitter, and I wished I could take it back. Instead, I cleared my throat and said, "Really. I'm fine—"

"Good. Because this guy I want you to meet is so hot! He's successful. Charming. Single."

I laughed at the last bit. "Single shouldn't be an enticing quality but, rather, a requirement."

Marie clucked her tongue against the roof of her mouth. "She's not ready!" she emphasized on my behalf, and I winced.

"But this guy will not stay on the market. I guarantee it," Jenn argued.

"Well, she doesn't need to rush." Marie's hands are on her hips now. She was five years older than me, but she assumed her significant sister role to the extent that I sometimes wondered if she was my mother in another universe.

My head bounced between my sisters while they discussed my love life.

"This is insane," I muttered, passing the bouquets to the other bridesmaids.

"Ten minutes!" the wedding planner, Lulu, called into the room.

One would assume my sister would have been a ball of nerves before she waltzed down the aisle and signed her life away to the love of her life, but no, she'd much rather berate my puny, pathetic, nonexistent one.

"You ready?" I asked, hoping to distract her from the topic.

She ignored me. "You won't miss him. He's like six-foot, with dark hair and dreamy eyes. He went to undergrad with Tony."

"Cool. But um…" I cleared my throat, nervous to say it out loud for fear that he wouldn't show up. "I actually have a date coming."

The entire room fell silent, and my sisters gaped at me.

"Anna Joy McKinley!" Marie scolded.

I blanched. "What?"

"Who?—"

"When?—"

"I knew you were smiling all weird and googly-eyed at your phone last night…" Marie shook her head.

"I was not—" I try to argue, but my cheeks flame and the memory of last night's kiss makes my lips tingle.

"Oh my God! Does Mom know?" Jenn asked.

"Know what?" Mom said as she poked her head in. She looked straight at her daughter dressed in white, and tears filled her eyes. "Oh, my baby girl! You are just prettier than a picture!" she gushed, dabbing her eyes.

"Oh, Mom! Don't cry! You'll make me cry," Jenn said as my mom embraced her by the elbows and rocked her side to side.

"Oh, my! Jenn, darling, you look all grown up," my dad said, entering the room in his three-piece suit.

"Mom! Anna said she is bringing someone to the wedding!" Marie practically hissed.

I scolded her with my eyes. "Timing, sis."

Mom and Dad looked at me. "Really? Why wasn't he here last night?" Dad asked.

"He had a parent-teacher conference," I explained, and my dad nodded, but Marie drew her head back.

"Single dad doesn't strike me as your type," she said, admiring her nails and feigning disinterest.

"Why not?" I was offended at first, but then I caught myself and shook my head. "No, he's a teacher. He drove up this morning."

Jenn flashed a pretentious smirk at Marie.

"What's his name? Where does he live?" Dad asked, and I shrunk down into my sixteen-year-old self again.

I took in a breath. "His name is Isaac Morrison, and he lives in Gig Harbor with me."

"*With you?*" my sisters shrieked in unison.

"Five minutes!" Lulu called into the room.

My eyes jerked toward Lulu, and when the door closed again, I realized all eyes were on me. "No, he doesn't live *with* me. But he also lives in Gig Harbor."

"How'd you meet?" Marie asked. She sounded like a snarky detective rather than an interested sister.

"Oh my God, can we discuss this later? You are literally about to walk down the aisle to get married," I pleaded, all while feeling vindicated in knowing my family would one hundred percent behave this way. "I'll tell you everything. And you'll meet him tonight. But, like, can Jenn go get married first?"

My mom laughed at this and squeezed me, then turned back to Jenn. "My baby is getting married!"

The bridesmaids lined up at the entrance to the Spanish Ballroom at the Fairmont, where my sister invited two-hundred-and-fifty of her closest friends to celebrate her marrying the one for her. I love that about weddings.

Stepping into the room was like stepping into a castle. Lush white flowers lined the aisle, and a white runner spread from the back to the front of the room where the altar stood just under an arched window.

Tony was fidgeting slightly at the end of the aisle, but his smile was sharp, and I could sense more joy than trepidation as I moved closer to him. As I neared the end of the aisle to take my place on the steps, my heart began to hammer, realizing I hadn't seen Isaac on my way down. I pressed my eyes closed and swallowed the nightmare of explaining why my "boyfriend" didn't show up to my sister's wedding after I promised them they'd all get to meet him.

When I opened my eyes, though, I found him right away. Dressed in a striking, fitted navy suit and adorned with his perfect smile, I still couldn't help but think he had the bluest eyes I'd ever seen. He was perfection, sitting in the sixth row next to Mr. and Mrs. Olson, who lived next door to us growing up. I wondered what he was thinking as he took in the sight of my family, my sisters, and every guest that warranted an invitation. If he was at all flustered, he didn't show it. Even how he looked at me and smiled as I walked back down the aisle after the vows were over fooled everyone who saw. Even me.

My heart fluttered, and my gut clenched because he looked at me like I was the only person in the room. I smiled back and suddenly couldn't wait to find him at the reception.

nine

NOW

I always thought about cheating on John.

But I mostly wondered if he would be the one to do it. I think a part of me wanted him to. I tempted him with each cold shoulder, every time I ignored him, every time I compared him to the life I actually wanted. I cornered him into breaking that vow, but he never did. At least, I never found out if he did. I thought it would make the end clear—a definitive he-did-this-so-we-had-to-get-a-divorce answer to the overly complex question of why.

Our families would have understood that. Our kids would have understood that.

Instead, our kids are faced with being told their five- and seven-year-old minds may not always understand grownup problems, but maybe one day, when they're older, they will. I look at Suzy as her legs swing under the gold Chiavari chair. Her eyes are filled with glee as she sips her sparkling cider from a plastic cup and watches her cousin dance with her groom for the first time as a married couple.

I smile at her and feel a tug on my dress, and I turn to Henry. "I need to go potty!"

I nod and start to stand, but John stops me, "I can take him."

"I want Mommy!" Henry yells, and I hush him softly. Our table is near the dance floor, and I don't want to disrupt the beautiful moment.

"It's fine," I whisper, taking Henry's hand.

"It's your niece, Anna; you should stay," John says—a hushed reprimand that makes my blood boil.

"She's your niece too." I enunciate each word with vigor and contempt, but the tone and breath in which the words come out would seem pleasant to anyone within earshot. I shoot my sister, Jenn, a smile as she narrows her eyes on me. "Come on, honey. Let's hurry," I say to Henry, and we escape the reception room and head down the hall to the restrooms.

Vineyard 1301 was a lovely choice for the reception. There aren't many tasting rooms in this area large enough to accommodate a wedding reception, but this one is perfect. It's a reclaimed barn, but the interior is sleek and bright in design. The reception room is stunning. The tall ceilings wrapped in twinkling lights and floral chandeliers make it feel like a summer night sky in the frost of February. White tablecloths cover the round tables surrounding the dance floor. Each one adorned with fresh flowers and candles. The gold chairs are wrapped in blush-colored silk, matching the sparkling rosé poured into each glass.

"The custom labels for the night's wine is a brilliant idea, don't you think?" Jenn asks as we take our seats back at the table. I stare at the bottle as she refills my glass. The label is blush pink with gold writing to match the colors of the wedding, and the label reads Raymond Rosé, a taste of Happily Ever After.

I smile at the bottle, then glance at Serene and Beau, the Raymonds, as they stroll from table to table, greeting their guests.

"It really is the sweetest idea," I answer.

"Marie said the owner is a complete romantic and does it for every wedding here. I mean, I'm sure the wine is the same as what they sell, but still, the custom labels are adorable."

"That's incredible," I agree, smiling fondly at the atmosphere my sister created for her daughter's special day.

"Serene ordered two cases to keep for anniversaries," Jenn adds, taking a bite of her salmon.

I raise my eyebrows and hum, stalling my following sentence by sipping my rosé. Two cases of wine are twenty-four bottles. I hope they make it there. I hope they surpass it. I hope they aren't like John and me, ten years in and regretting the last four.

John squeezes my knee. It's an apology. Regardless of how terrible we were to each other in recent years, we never stopped knowing each other. It's a direct correlation from living with someone for over a decade. I glance at him and shrug.

He holds my gaze for a few moments. It's like he wants to kiss me. He looks like he wants to correct his wrongs or forgive my trespasses. Or maybe we already have, and we're sitting here in purgatory at our niece's wedding because the timing is terrible to tell our families we're getting a divorce.

I can practically hear them asking why, with tears in their eyes and desperation etched on their foreheads. "But you two are so good together," they'll say. "Why would you give up now?"

Because we didn't love each other enough, and we don't want to.

ten

THEN

"You look good," I said, making a beeline straight for him at the bar.

"You look better," he responded, holding my hand out and making me twirl.

The bridesmaid dress my sister chose wasn't awful, but the light shade of blue wasn't my first choice. The hourglass cut of the gown made up for the lackluster color, along with the plunging back and scooped neckline. As I spun, my curled hair draped over my bare shoulder.

"Thank you," I said, smiling. He took me by the waist, brushing my hair over my shoulder. As he did this, his knuckles brushed against the scar on my shoulder.

"You have a scar," he said.

"Oh, yeah. Curling iron when I was fifteen. Jenn did it by

accident." I waved my hand with a laugh.

He didn't respond right away. He ran his thumb over the scar twice, bent down, and kissed it gently. "Those evil sisters of yours," he muttered. "Let's make them crazy tonight."

I grinned. "Can't wait."

"Now," he said, sipping his red wine and scanning the reception room. "What do I need to know? Do you have touchy relatives? A weird great aunt that will hit on me?"

I drew back as I giggled into my champagne. "You wish."

His gaze swept over me, not in a grossly obvious way, but in a way that made me feel like he was holding back. Not from hitting on me like a typical dirtbag I met in a bar, but it was as if there was a question in his gaze. A wondering. A daydream I was starring in.

I tried not to let it get the best of me, disguised my desire to return the gaze with information.

"Oh, yes. The rundown," I began, glancing around the hotel ballroom. "See that lady with the floral pantsuit?" He nodded. "She'll ask your political affiliation within twenty seconds of the meeting. And her husband will sneak in ways to ask you to donate to his campaign." He tsked out a laugh.

"Aren't politics taboo to talk about at a wedding?"

"Aren't they taboo to talk about at any gathering involving blood relatives?" I countered, and he smirked.

"Okay, who else?"

"Oh! That's my cousin, Millie. She works in HR, though, I'm pretty sure she moonlights as a celebrity gossip social media account. She will know your deepest, darkest status from 2014 within fifteen minutes of getting your full name."

He throws his head back and laughs. "Well, that sounds useful."

I snapped my face to his. "Don't you dare say your real name."

"I won't. I'm Isaac Morrison through and through," he responded, and I laughed.

"Yes, it suits you." I smiled at him, and then spotted my mother's best friend, Denise, frowning at us. My shoulder blades pinched back, and a nervous chill drummed up my neck.

"What's wrong?" he asked, sipping his drink and scanning the crowd. The tension in my shoulders released as I realized how quickly he read me.

"Nothing—ummm, well, it's about my ex," I began, my eyes dropping to the parquet floor and when they landed back on Isaac, he was reaching for me, cupping a hand around my jaw and he leaned down to whisper in my ear.

"So we need to make him crazy jealous?" The breath from his mouth heated the skin below my ear, and goosebumps rose on my flesh. His other hand traveled down my ribcage toward my hip.

I tilted my head back and reluctantly admitted, "He's not here."

Isaac grinned, swiping a thumb against the hinge of my jaw. I sensed him preparing to let go, so I quickly added, "But this—I like this." I cleared my throat, clarifying. "This is believable."

His hand moved down my neck to my shoulder, and he kissed my forehead. My eyes fell closed. He was so tender, so thoughtful with each of his movements that I felt my heart swooning without permission.

"So, tell me, Anna. Why are we mentioning your ex if he isn't here? If he's occupying that pretty little mind of yours, I might start to get jealous," he whispered before pulling his lips from my ear. The scent of his cologne lingered, making me feel hypnotized.

My gaze floated toward his. "You'd really get jealous?" He wet his lips, but before he could speak, I shook my head out of the clouds and answered. "I mean, it's not that he's occupying my mind, per se. It's just that almost everyone knows about the broken engagement because half of these guests were once invited to my wedding, which didn't happen."

Clarity was written in his gaze as soon as I revealed the information, but instead of getting weirded out, he spun me around so my back was to his chest in a protective embrace, nuzzling close. The rough scrape of his stubble against my cheek made me want to kiss him and run my hand against it. I restrained myself as he spoke, "Ah, who cares? He probably had it coming."

I smirked up at him. "How do you know he wasn't the one who called it off?"

Isaac turned me around, his presence nearly swallowing me whole. "Because I'm looking at you, and there is not a man on this earth who wouldn't beg you not to break his heart."

I let out a breath of a laugh and fidgeted with the stem of my glass. "Yeah, well, a good portion of this room thinks I let a good one get away, so—"

"Do you think that?"

I stared up at his deep blue eyes, wondering how he asked the right questions that cut straight to the core of the matter. "Are you sure you aren't a therapist?"

"I'm a teacher, same difference."

"And a snitch," I added with a sneer.

"Mandatory reporter," he corrected with an expression that walked the line between wanting to strangle me and carry me away.

"Same difference."

"You aren't answering my question."

"Which was?"

"Do you think you let a good one get away?"

I drew in a long breath, buying time to come up with an answer. "I think he was a good one. But I think he wasn't the one for me."

He nodded as if that settled it. "So everyone else can fuck off. It's your life, Anna. You're the one that has to live it."

These were simple words I had heard over and over from self-help books and tiny squares on Instagram, but that night, coming from his lips, they hit me square in the heart. A slow smile spread over my lips. "I feel like I could kiss you."

The right side of his mouth pulled slightly, revealing a

dimple, and I reached out and brushed my thumb over it. "You should," he whispered. "It's the only way people will believe us."

As I tossed my head back and laughed, I saw Marie gaping at us from the corner of my eye. I averted my eyes quickly, but it was too late. I knew she was heading straight for us.

He licked his lips and nodded. "You're uncomfortable."

My eyes flitted back to him. "No, I'm fine."

"You are. What's wrong? Embarrassed to say you know me?"

"No!" I nearly shouted, then calmed my voice. "No, I—" I cleared my throat. "I'm worried we won't pull this off."

Marie placed her champagne on a table, grabbed her husband by the arm, and marched straight for us.

"My sister is coming," I warned.

He raised his glass, pointing at her from across the room. "Her?"

I grabbed his elbow and yanked him toward me. "God, you are a child."

"That's offensive."

I rolled my eyes. "Don't be so sensitive, or you'll never last in my family."

He grinned. "Oh, I hope I get the chance to prove you wrong. I could last in your family."

"I've known you for twenty-four hours," I retorted.

"And yet, it feels so much longer," he whispered.

"I don't even know your parents' names." The panic was rising in my blood the closer my sister got to us. I took a long sip of champagne.

"I'm an orphan."

I coughed out the champagne, gathering the attention of virtually everyone around us.

"I'm joking. I doubt my parents' names will even come up," he laughed. He rubbed my upper arm softly. "Anna, you have to relax."

"Oh, God, I really did not think this through." I breathed

a sigh of relief, and he dabbed my chin with his napkin, then slid his thumb under my lip to straighten my lipstick. "This is the first time I've introduced someone since my engagement ended." I drew in a slow breath, steadying my nerves. In any other circumstance, I loved being single—except when it came to my sisters.

He kissed my temple, murmuring, "Relax. This will be fun."

"Are you going to introduce your friend?" Marie asked when she reached us, a smile plastered on her face.

I cleared my throat. "Of course. This is Isaac Morrison. Isaac, this is my sister Marie and her husband, Daniel."

Marie held out her hand. "Dr. McKinley-Watkins."

My lip snarled in disgust as my eyes darted between them, but Isaac didn't flinch. "Pleasure to meet you, Dr. McKinley-Watkins." Then he turned to Daniel.

"Ah, call me Danny."

I wanted to say, absolutely no one wants to call a grown-ass adult Danny, but I refrained.

Isaac unleashed a smile that had quickly become my favorite in the world and said, "Nice to meet you, Danny."

"Is this the man of the hour?" Jenn shouted, wading through the crowd to us in her ridiculously oversized wedding gown.

I smiled at her. "And this is my sister, Jenn."

"Look how handsome!" she exclaimed as she wrapped her arms around Isaac and rocked him back and forth in an overbearing hug. "Come to fix the brokenhearted sister, have you?"

He chuckled, humorless yet charming, as he reared back. "I think your sister is the one doing the fixing."

Jenn waved a hand. "Nonsense. We've been trying to get this one to get over her ex for years!"

"It's only been two years," I countered, but I was certain no one heard.

"Oh please, Jenn. You know Anna isn't ever going to be over him," Marie huffed, and I watched Daniel tighten his grip on her arm as a warning.

"Marie, that's…" I shook my head, stunned. I didn't know what to say. I knew what I wanted to say: that's fucked up. Uncalled for. Disrespectful. Untrue. But the words seized up in my throat. I hated that she said this. I hated the preposterous edge in her voice. I hated that every word she said wasn't bad when it was just ink on paper, but the tone, the expression, and her eyes filled with pity all made me feel like a stray dog they shooed away at brunch. My chest tightened as I remembered there was nothing like a wedding to highlight my singleness. Even with someone as handsome as Isaac Morrison on my arm, my sisters didn't care. I would always be the one that never got anything quite right.

"Well, this is a start!" Jenn said. "It's so good to meet you, Isaac."

"You too. The wedding was lovely. Congratulations," Isaac said.

"Thank you. I better go find my *husband*!" she squealed. "We have rounds to make."

I smiled and watched her walk away. When my eyes landed back on Marie, she looked entirely confused, examining me with this man called Isaac. Awareness prickled at my senses, and I worried she knew we were faking it.

"So, how long has this been going on?" Marie asked.

Isaac raised my hand to his lips. "Not long enough," he said, and my heart fluttered.

Marie nodded, and Daniel said, "What do you do?"

"I'm a teacher," Isaac answered. I smiled proudly at him.

"Nice." Daniel slurped his bourbon.

"Well, the bouquet and garter toss will be in a few minutes," Marie said, glancing at her wrist that didn't have a watch. I tried not to roll my eyes. "You'll be out there, I assume."

"Oh yes, we are nearly thirty years old and absolutely dying to let the toss of wedding props decide our fate," I said.

Marie winced.

I thought about sticking out my tongue at her but

restrained myself from being so juvenile, just as I felt Isaac's fingertips brush against my cheek, brushing a loose curl away from my face.

"I can't wait," he said. "But, if you'll excuse us, we must go find your parents. Have you seen them?"

Daniel and Marie pointed across the room, and we excused ourselves from my big sister's torture.

"That wasn't so bad," I murmured when we were out of earshot.

"No, you were drowning in nerves. I saw it, and that is simply not who you are," he replied.

I tilted my head in his direction. "You're so encouraging and, also, you don't know me. Drowning in nerves is my specialty regarding awkward social encounters."

He paused at the outskirts of the reception room, staring down at me with hooded eyes and soft lips. "I may not know you now. But I will. It's my mission to get to know you."

I bit my lip to contain my smile, and he moved closer to my face, pressing me against a white pillar. "You need to relax. Get whatever tension it is winding you out of your system."

I swallowed hard, nerves rattling in my gut like marbles on a wood floor. "Do you understand how many eyes are on me tonight?"

I flashed a side-long glance at the wedding guests surrounding us and he immediately tilted my chin back to face him. The refocus made me exhale just as it made something pinch down low in my belly.

"Oh, so you think you're important? Trying to upstand the bride?"

I let out a laugh, releasing the tension. "No, I mean… people are going to talk about the handsome teacher who couldn't take his hands off Anna at her sister's wedding."

"Isn't that the point of all this?" he whispered. As he moved closer, I knew he was right. That was the point. He tucked his fingers in my hair, and I felt the tension in my body release into his hands. "If you don't want me to kiss you, just say it."

"Isaac," I breathed out with a laugh, heat hitting my cheeks as I glanced around us again.

"I like it when you call me that." His grin deepened, and I realized I liked it, too. I enjoyed creating a version of us in a bubble. It was like we painted this picture of who we were together in a different dimension, and no one knew about it but us.

"My sister is watching." I swallowed hard.

"Good. She should stop pitying you and realize you belong on a pedestal. Untouchable. Untamable. And everything I ever dreamed of." I knew it was a part of the act, but it was like his words pressed pause. I absorbed what he was saying and realized how much I had been told how sorry everyone felt for me. How everyone thought I was the broken one who lost the love of my life. Isaac ran his thumb along my jaw until it touched my chin. "Do you want me to stop?"

"No," I breathed. "Please just kiss me."

He unleashed a smile when I said that before sinking his lips into mine. It was only our second kiss, but damn, it felt achingly familiar. It was the kind of kiss that fell over my entire body, making my toes tingle. I loved the way he held my face in his hands. I loved the way he tasted. I loved how butterflies erupted in my stomach, making me feel like I was floating away on their wings.

He pulled back, then kissed me once more—just a soft peck on my lips, then again on my forehead.

"We shouldn't get carried away before dinner is even served," I whispered.

He chewed on his lip and nodded with a shy smile. "You're right. This could get very out of hand."

I nodded, unable to stop smiling. I broke eye contact and took his hand to lead him to the head table, and introduced him to my parents.

eleven

NOW

"At this time, ladies and gentlemen, I'd like to invite all the married couples to the dance floor," the DJ announces.

I stay put, wiping the buttercream frosting off Henry's chin while Suzy taste-tests each decadent dessert.

"Come on! Let's go! Did you hear him, Anna?" Serene asks, with Beau holding her waist.

"Oh, I'm not one for dancing," I answer, waving a hand and turning back to Suzy. "How's the red velvet?"

"Not as good as the lemon," she says with complete assurance.

"You sure? Let me try." I open my mouth for a bite, and Jenn says, "When have you ever *not been one for dancing?!*"

I laugh, licking cream cheese frosting off my lips. "I don't even know where John is right now."

She points over my shoulder. "He's right there. Come on, *Auntie Anna,* get your dancing shoes on."

I swallow hard as John approaches. I don't want to dance with him. Not when we're discussing meetings with our lawyer to dissolve this mistake once and for all.

"Dance with me, Anna," John says, holding a hand out to me with a somber expression. "One last time."

"Yeah, Mommy, dance!" Henry squeals.

I smile at my son fondly, but as I do, something in my chest twists. He's the victim in all of this, and so is his sister. I don't, even for a moment, regret having either of my children. They are precious gifts that have taught me more about life than anyone. But I also know they will hurt when we tell them Mommy and Daddy aren't going to be married anymore.

John leads me to the floor and takes me in his arms— strong, safe, familiar. There is so much about him I wonder if I'll miss. But I don't wonder if I'll miss him enough to regret the split.

"This has been a beautiful wedding," he says.

I nod as I look out at the room. It's breathtaking. The flowers. The silk. The music. The wine. The dancing. The gown. The promises.

"Marie and Danny are probably so proud."

"They are," I agree, trying to meet his eyes. But he keeps his gaze fixed past my shoulder. Every movement or touch today may seem intimate to onlookers but I know he hasn't looked me in the eye since he asked for a divorce last night.

We're done with small moments of intimacy. We're done with private moments of understanding. We're done trying. We're done pretending.

"If you've been married for one day or less, please make your way off the dance floor," the DJ announces and the guests roar in applause as Serene and Beau leave the dance.

We stay put.

The song continues to play.

"If you have been married one year or less, please leave

the dance floor!"

A few couples leave the dance floor, reminding me how much getting married right after college is par for the course—the rule not the exception. As I sway methodically with John, I watch the young, fresh-faced twenty-three-year-olds return to their tables and cocktails.

"Five years or less, love birds!" the DJ prompts, and more people leave the dance floor.

We stay painfully put.

"If you have been married for ten years or less, please make your way off the dance floor!" the DJ announces.

Relief floods my chest. I hate faking it. I always have. I want every moment of affection and intimacy to be authentic—whether it be dancing at a wedding or kissing under the stars.

We pause and separate as we make our way off the dance floor. But just before we reach our children at the table, he runs a finger down the back of my arm, gaining my attention.

"I'm sorry, Anna," he whispers.

I'm tired of the line. I'm tired of forgiveness. I'm just tired of explaining. "I know, John," I say. "I know."

I step away, let out a low breath, and make my way outside to the patio for some fresh air. Stepping off that dance floor felt like a final step. The last time we'd dance, knowing the last time we truly loved each other was years ago. People often say you get one shot at love. It's not true. There are many. Some last for a lifetime. Others for just a night.

I breathe in as the memory washes over me. It was so long ago, yet I can still taste the wine and the kisses. I can still feel him brush my hair over my shoulder and run his fingers down my back. I let out a small laugh to myself. There's no way he remembers the way I do.

I turn around to head back inside, and time stills when I first see him because I'm not quite sure it's really him. Between the years and the champagne, not to mention the context, my mind can't fathom how it's him or why he'd even be here.

But when his deep blue eyes meet mine, I'm certain it's really him.

twelve

THEN

"This is the best night of my life!" my father said.

I laughed as Isaac took another shot with him and my sister, Jenn's new husband, Joseph.

"What. Is. Happening?" my mother came over, cheeks flushed, hands on her hips, and an astonished smile.

"We love him!" Joseph said, slinging an arm over my fake boyfriend.

"He's pretty great," my mother agreed. I caught the gaze of Marie, whose jaw was tight and her eyes narrowed.

I knew it was because Isaac didn't fit the mold of anyone I had ever dated. He was more handsome. More fun. More friendly. All of it was so much easier, even if it was all pretend.

"Excuse me, gentlemen," he said to my father and

brother-in-law, then turned to me, "And my lady. I have to find Aunt Marla. I promised her a dance." He held a hand to his chest and winked at me before stepping away and dancing with my eight-two-year-old great aunt.

"This is for real?" Marie asked, entirely skeptical.

I rolled my eyes. "Please stop analyzing and let me have fun tonight."

"It's just… you never mentioned anyone, and you two seem like you've been together for years," she explained and I chewed on my lip, unsure what to say. "I mean, I guess when you know, you know, but…" She shook her head like she was trying to wrap her brain around her sister having a boyfriend she never knew about who seemed crazy about her.

"I've decided not to overthink it and just enjoy it. We're having fun together. No long-term commitment or anything… just fun, and it's working," I answered with a shrug.

"Right, but…" Marie hesitated. "He seems like a lot of fun now, but one day, down the road, you're going to need someone to ground you. Keep you steady, you know?"

I narrowed my eyes on my sister. I knew what she meant, but I didn't want that. "I'm not looking for someone to keep me on the ground right now. I very much prefer flying."

"Well, maybe one day, you'll need that."

I nodded, trying to ignore her message as she walked away. But I knew better. Deep down, I knew I'd need someone to keep me steady one day. I turned to the bartender. "Shot of tequila, please?"

"Make that two," a low voice said next to me, tucking a couple of twenties in the tip jar. He smiled down at me. Tall, dark hair, disarming smile. "Are you having fun tonight?"

"I am," I answered. "This might just be my favorite wedding I've ever attended."

He chuckled. "I'm happy to hear that. How do you know the bride and groom?"

"The bride is my sister."

His eyes swiped down my dress, and he recognized the

light blue silk of the wedding party. "Oh, duh. I should have been paying closer attention."

I waved a hand in the air. "Ah, no worries. This entire room is a blend of white Spanish molding, gold chandeliers, and blue silk. After a few drinks, we all blend together."

He laughed at that, more or less to be polite, but the way he lingered told me he was interested. I searched the dance floor for Isaac to no avail.

"Oh, you've met!" Jenn said, coming up next to me.

"I'm sorry?" I asked.

"This is the guy I told you about that I wanted you to meet," she answered.

I nodded slowly. "Oh, well—"

"Yeah, I know, she's here with somebody, so don't get any ideas, but you can still meet. And maybe one day…" her shoulders did a little shimmy at what she was implying.

I froze, and the man let out a low laugh, diffusing the implications from my sister. "I'm John," he said, holding out his hand.

I shook it. "I'm Anna. It's nice to meet you."

"Pleasure is all mine," he said with a nod.

"Well, maybe I'll see you around," I said, not wanting to linger in the conversation. It didn't matter that he was handsome or seemed nice enough; the whole façade of Isaac Morrison and me would crumble if I even entertained a conversation. But if I was frank with myself, I didn't even want to. I tried to run back to Isaac's arms, even if it was just for the night.

So I went. And I danced with Isaac until we sent off the happy couple under a downpour of glitter and confetti. I smiled over my shoulder at Isaac, and he caught my face in his hands before I turned away.

He kissed me for the ninth time in our lives—I counted each one throughout the night, savoring the delicacy on my tongue. But this time, everything inside me twisted and pulled and heated like a winding spool of passion and I was ready for him, this familiar stranger, to unravel me.

"You ready to leave?" I asked, pulling away.

He raised his smug eyebrows, his lips curling into a slow smile. "Oh, we're really doing this."

I stepped away from him slowly, my fingers lingering on the buttons of his shirt. "You talk a big game, *Isaac*. Don't tell me it was all for nothing."

He licked his lips and nodded. "I just want you to be sure. No pressure. We can leave it at this."

I shook my head. "Come on. My room is just upstairs."

His hand stayed in mine as we made our way to the elevator. As soon as the doors dinged closed, his hands were in my hair, and his lips were on mine. We stumbled down the hallway to my hotel room, fumbling with the key card, kicking off our shoes, and pulling at each other's clothes.

I had nothing but want rushing through my veins. He was the needle. I was the vein. I was prepared to be marked and scarred and played with until I was ragged in the dead of night. All I wanted was him in every way I could have him.

There was a recklessness in faking it—an irresponsibility of not promising tomorrow. We created this fantasy inside a glass dome and I wanted to live out every part of it.

I tore open his shirt and knelt before him as the buttons of his shirt scattered across the hotel carpet.

"I've always wanted to do that," I admitted.

He grinned down at me, but only slightly. A dark, predatory look clouded over his blue eyes like a storm in the night. I held his stare as I unbuckled his belt, undid the button of his pants, and slid down the zipper. I pulled him out of his boxers and licked the tip, and he moaned.

"You are unreal," he breathed.

His voice turned me on so much it was almost embarrassing. He only had his hands in my hair, but I could feel him all over my skin, burning and pulsing in all the right ways.

I wanted to be disrespected, devoured, and cherished all at the same time.

But as I took him in my mouth as far as I could, the deep

growl that hissed through his teeth made me want to keep pleasuring him until he was saying my name.

He gripped my hair tighter and tossed his head back. "Fuck, Anna."

I kept going. I never particularly enjoyed this act of floor play, but for some reason, with Isaac, I couldn't stop, I couldn't get enough—not until he was spilling down my throat.

I sat back on my heels and looked up at him with a delirious smile on my face as I swiped my bottom lip with my thumb. His chest rose and fell with each heavy breath, bringing him down. He let out a low laugh before beckoning me to stand before him. I rose slowly with his finger under my chin.

"Anna, that wasn't fair," he whispered, deep and throaty. "I haven't even gotten to see you yet."

A euphoric laugh escaped my lips as he backed me into the central part of the hotel room. When we stopped, we were standing at the end of the bed. His undone pants were slung at his waist, and his shirt was open. I was shoeless with smeared lipstick but otherwise wholly dressed.

"First," he began, slipping my dress over my shoulders. "I'm going to take this off. Then I will admire every freckle on your skin and every curve of your body." He flicked the last of the fabric over my shoulder, and the delicate material fell and pooled at my feet. "Then I will touch you in every way I possibly can. Then, I will make you say my name like you just made me say yours. And if you don't want any of that, I need you to tell me now."

I smiled at him as he gingerly brushed his fingertips under the lace of my panties. "And here I thought you were going to surprise me," I teased, then inhaled sharply as his fingertips touched me, swallowing my words as my legs weakened at his touch.

The movement was soft and circular and perfect. I clung to his shirt and pulled it off him. I needed every piece of clothing off of both of us… immediately. There was a primal need to feel his skin against mine no matter what regret may hit me the following day.

I didn't care, not about anything.

Except him.

Within moments, we were bare, face to face and skin to skin. He danced his fingertips on my body, finding the freckle on my shoulder. He kissed it once. He traced his finger to the next one on my chest and kissed it, too. Then to my belly. Then, he moved over to my hip and around to the middle of my back. He traced each freckle like he was charting constellations. It made the moment far more intimate than anything I would have ever expected. It was like he wanted to commit me to his memory.

And I hoped he did. I hoped he found precisely what space in his mind I would occupy for years to come.

"Lie down, Anna," he said, and I didn't hesitate.

He hovered over me, kissing my hip bones, my navel, my chest, my neck. My throat hitched as I felt him position himself above me in a way I knew that everything I wanted was about to happen. But before I felt the pressure I so desperately needed, he spoke.

"What do you want, Anna? I'll give it to you. Just tell me," he whispered against the skin just below my ear.

My fingers curled into his back as I pulled him closer. "I want you to make this so good, I never forget. Months, years, decades from now. I want the memory of tonight to be something I'll never forget."

He pulled back so I could see his eyes, hooded and determined.

I wish I could say the rest was a blur, but it's all a vivid memory, alive and replaying in my mind.

Every touch, every taste, every turn, every movement, every moan, every word, every time I said his name. I knew it was only for one night, so I treasured all of it and hoped I'd never forget.

And the same for him. I wanted him to remember me. I wanted him to remember that for one weekend, we pretended to love each other, and somehow, it would become one of my favorite memories for years to come.

Afterward, I laid on his bare shoulder, tracing a languid finger from his chest hair down his abdomen.

"What is your real name?" I asked.

"Oh, now you want to know my real name? After you've been yelling my fake one." He laughed, and I buried my face in my hands.

"I think we decided your name was Isaac before you could be anything else," I admitted. "But honestly, it worked because I didn't call you the wrong name once."

He smiled down at me and kissed my forehead. "It's Isaac."

My jaw dropped. "Stop it."

"I'm serious," he laughed.

"Liar." No part of me believed him.

"I'm telling the truth. Grab my wallet; I'll show you my driver's license."

I studied him momentarily, wondering if I should, but curiosity always kills the cat, so I grabbed his wallet and pulled out his driver's license.

"You had me all figured out," he commented, and I smiled so wide my cheeks hurt.

"Isaac Brooks," I read, then bit my bottom lip. "Sorry, your last name was way off."

"It's all good." He smiled at me in that sleepy, just-sexed way, making my stomach flutter.

I replaced his driver's license and tossed his wallet back on the bedside table, then crawled back to him, "Well, Mr. Brooks, it is lovely to properly meet you."

A rough chuckle tumbled out of his pretty mouth as I curled into his side, and he held me against his chest. "Anna, it has been an absolute pleasure to meet you."

"You know what I want to do?" I asked, running a finger down his chest.

He cocked a suggestive eyebrow at me.

"Not that—I mean, yes. But also, I really want to order a

pizza."

He smiled wide, reached for his phone, and immediately started punching in an order. "What's your favorite kind of pizza?"

"Based on how well we're getting along this weekend, probably the same as yours," I said.

We stared at each other for a beat then both immediately said: "Meat lovers."

Laughter exploded out of us.

"Ranch?" he asked.

"No!" I shrieked. "That ruins pizza."

He shook his head and clicked his tongue against the roof of his mouth. "You were almost perfect."

I giggled. "I won't judge you for ranch on pizza if you don't judge me for liking pineapple on pizza."

"Now I feel like you're trying to start a war," he deadpanned and I laughed again while he went back to ordering pizza. "All right, what else?"

I sighed. Happy. Euphoric. "Just a little bit more of you."

He clicked *complete order* on his phone and a devilish grin flashed across his face as he rolled me on my back. "We have thirty minutes."

And that was when he gave me a little bit more of him.

Everything inside me melted and pulsed as he dragged his lips down my chest until his head was between my legs, and I was seeing stars.

Then we ate pizza and laughed through the night. We told each other our dreams—even the small ones that could be accomplished in a day, but also the big ones that could only be accomplished in a lifetime. I told him I wanted to own my own bookstore and he told me he wanted to one day own a winery.

"So do it," I said, and he shrugged.

"Maybe one day it will make sense."

I wiped my mouth with a napkin and took a sip of Diet Coke. "I don't think it's about doing it when it makes sense. I think it's about doing it because there's a passion inside you, fueling you to pursue it. If we wait to do things when they make sense, we'll be waiting forever."

"Or we'll only do the things that make sense and end up bored," he added.

"Or that," I agreed with a smile.

We stared at each other for a few moments before he spoke.

"So, after this weekend, I—" he began, but I cut him off, wanting to alleviate any of his concerns that I was clingy. Settling down was the last thing on my mind. And while the weekend with him was perfect, I didn't want to force a relationship, especially one that developed from trying to appease my sisters.

"Let's just leave it this way, really," I said. "I feel like we're just playing pretend, and I'm okay just leaving it at that. I don't want to force something and wind up in a boring marriage, living a boring life. I want to be able to tell people how we met and had a beautiful time. And how now, we'll have one of the most amazing stories to tell."

The words left my mouth before I could process what I was telling him. But for a split second, I found myself terrified of the road less traveled. The road I had been running down full speed with my wandering heart seemed like it would crumble at my feet one day at the hands of this man. I didn't want that. I wanted whatever he and I had to stay just like this: perfect and untouched.

He pressed his lips together, waiting a moment before responding. "Will I ever get to see you again?"

I shrugged, leaning down to kiss him. "Some things we will never know."

"Promise me one thing," he whispered.

"What?"

"That even if I call you and you don't answer, you'll never forget me."

thirteen

NOW

"Anna McKinley."

I don't correct him when he uses my maiden name, I smile and say, "What is Isaac *Morrison* doing at another McKinley wedding?"

"Brooks," he corrects, and I laugh, walking toward him. He finishes what he was saying to a staff member, then turns to me, still with the bluest eyes I've ever seen. "To what do I owe the pleasure?"

"I was going to ask the same thing," I say.

"Well, considering you're at my winery..." he trails, and my mouth drops.

"Vineyard 1301 is yours?" I ask, and he nods. "What happened to teaching?"

He lets out a small laugh. "I met this girl who told me she

didn't want to force something and wind up living a boring life, so I quit teaching, sold my house, and bought this place ten years ago." He grins as the memory of my own words hits me.

"Well, teaching is not a boring profession," I argue.

"Definitely not. But it was exhausting, and I didn't want to do it anymore. Best decision I ever made."

I smile. "I'm proud of you."

"Come here," he says, pulling me into his arms. I've only spent a total of thirty-six hours with him, and I haven't seen him in twelve years, but he still feels so familiar. His scent filling my lungs, his arms wrapped around me, the cadence of his breath, the sound of his laugh. It was a fever dream I woke up from twelve years ago, yet I can still hear the music we danced to. I can still taste his kiss. By the way, the embrace is lingering a few moments too long, which tells me the memories are flooding his mind, too. I pull back, knowing my estranged but very much legal husband is just inside.

"It's my niece's wedding," I say.

"Wait. Serene Watkins is the daughter of Dr. McKinley-Watkins?" he teases, and I scrunch my nose.

"She's not as pretentious as she used to be, but I'm shocked you didn't remember her," I say.

He runs a hand down his face and laughs. "I apologize for not realizing. My wedding coordinator, Cristina, takes care of all the events. I take care of the wine."

"Yes, I've heard. Both my sisters and niece are quite taken by you and how you designed special labels for the newlyweds. I think that's really sweet."

"Thank you," he says, nodding. He looks out at the field surrounding his tasting room. The sun is setting, music is buzzing from inside, and I have a million things I want to tell him, but I have no idea where to start. "You been good, Anna?"

I've held myself together for hours at this point—years, if we're being honest—but all it takes is the right person asking with the right tone to make the veneer protecting my heart crack.

"I've been better. But I'm okay," I admit.

His brow twists, and his lips twitch. "I don't like that answer."

"Well," I breathe. "Maybe I should have taken my own advice that you took all those years ago."

He nods slowly, understanding without knowing. But I'm sure he can see it written all over my face. He can see it in my stylish yet appropriate dress. My moderate makeup and my reasonably sized heels. I'm sure he can see it in the purse of my lips and the cinch of my shoulders. Years ago, I settled into a boring life with someone who is kind and worthy but doesn't know how to love me.

"You never called me back," he says finally.

"Have you held it against me?"

He smiles. "I've been bitter for years."

I press my lips together, biting back a smile, unsure what to say because I wish I had answered when he called. I hope I hadn't convinced myself it was a fever dream that could never be replicated. Because now, twelve years, two kids, and ten years of marriage later, he still crosses my mind.

Even during the good years John and I had. Because we did have those. Even when John and I fell madly in love. Because we did that, too. But even in all the good, there was always something in my twisted human emotions beckoning me back to the night I spent at the Fairmont Hotel in a room with a man whose name I had guessed but didn't know.

"I'm sorry I didn't call you back," I confess with a breath, then step closer as I speak. "Maybe one day—"

"Mommy!" Suzy squeals as she leaps into me, wrapping her arms around my waist. Henry follows.

I let out a laugh as Isaac smiles at my children, no doubt assessing all the ways time can be measured. In children. In professions. In homes. In morning coffee and midnight kisses. In moments and in memories.

"Isaac, these are my kids, Suzy and Henry."

Isaac squats down to high-five them. Henry high-fives

him back, and Suzy curtsies, so he laughs and then bows.

"Daddy said it's time to go," Suzy informs me.

My brow twists, knowing the party has just begun. But of course, John wants to leave and get the kids home and in bed at a reasonable hour. Heaven forbid we veer off our routine at our niece's wedding.

"Anna, I'm going to pull the car around." John appears in the doorway and then realizes I'm speaking to someone. "Hi there, John Collins."

Isaac shakes John's outstretched hand, and I'm confident this is actually the fever dream. "Isaac Brooks."

"He owns the winery." I nearly wince at my watered-down answer.

"Oh, nice. Well, the wedding has been amazing. Thank you." John turns to me. "Be at the car in five?"

I nod, pressing my lips together as he takes our kids' hands back through the reception room. I turn back to Isaac, and I can tell he just watched the interaction with curious eyes. I know he saw how cold it was. There was no kiss. No hand on my back. No touching. Just pure ice in our expressions.

"You good?" he asks, the memory of his voice vibrating over me.

"I haven't been good in years." I laugh, then tuck a strand of my hair being blown away in the wind behind my ear. "We're getting a divorce—just saving face for the sake of my niece."

Isaac nods. "I'm sorry."

"I'm not." I laugh again, relief flooding my bones. "I'm really not. It has been a long time coming."

He steps closer to me. "I want to say the right thing right now, and I'm not sure I know how."

"It's okay, Isaac. Truly. I didn't expect to see you, and you didn't expect to see me…" my voice falters over my words because I don't know how to say what I'm truly feeling.

"Right," he agrees. "But maybe one day…"

"Yeah, maybe." I smile, understanding his implication

while thinking, *I hope so.* "I promised I wouldn't forget you, Isaac. I kept that promise."

His blue eyes glisten in the twinkling lights strung over the patio. He smiles and says, "You'll be okay, Anna. People like you don't take life lightly. They soak up every last bit of it. I don't know you as well as I want to, but there was a fire in you that was hard to miss."

I grin, realizing that the whirlwind of a weekend together meant just as much to him as it did to me.

"Thank you, Isaac," I answer. "Maybe one day I'll call you."

His expression lights up. "If I should only be so lucky."

fourteen

THEN

The door to the bookstore where I worked chimed, and I knew exactly who it was.

We were about to close, but Shelby, who worked there on Wednesdays and Fridays after school, said an "Isaac Brooks" would stop by to pick up his order.

Initially, I was confused hearing his name regarding a book order because that was a made-up scenario. It wasn't real life, and it was eight months ago.

Sure enough, after he reached out to me for the third time, Isaac ordered books for his classroom.

I glanced up from the counter to see his bright smile and confident disposition. "Well, well, well... look what the cat dragged in," I said, smiling.

As he walked toward me, I realized his hair was longer,

and his facial hair was more pronounced than it was, but when he flashed a familiar smile, I felt like he looked exactly the same.

"That is a very fifty-year-old dad thing to say," he teased, approaching me.

I laughed. "Well, I'll admit I thought of about ten different things I could say to you when I saw you for the first time in eight months, and that was the best I could do."

"I highly doubt that was the best of your options."

"Well, I considered, who let this guy in? But that didn't make sense because it's I'm the only one working."

He laughed as he moved closer, bracing the counter and towering over me. I forgot how all-consuming being in his presence could feel. He had one of those magnetic personalities. The kind that takes up all the space and absorbs all the oxygen, and yet, I didn't mind.

"I've come to collect something that's mine," he said, staring down at me.

My heart somersaulted in my chest before I realized what he was talking about.

"Right. Your books," I said, dropping to my knees to the box with a yellow Post-It that read Isaac Brooks on it. I grabbed the box and hoisted it on the counter with a loud thud, then blew my hair out of my face.

I had all day to prepare to see him, but I was still visibly flustered. I could feel the heat bloom over my chest, neck, and cheeks. The way his gaze dropped from my eyes made me wonder if he was counting how many hives were appearing on the tender skin of my neck.

"Thank you for the support, really." I nodded and swallowed hard. "We've barely been hanging on these days, so anytime anyone makes a large order like this, it means the world to me."

He shifted the box toward him, and I ignored my desire to look at his hands.

"Of course," he said. "How have you been?"

I opened my mouth and closed it, letting the drumming in

my heart consume my thoughts. "I've been good. You?"

"Good," he said. He paused for a moment and then stuffed a hand in his pocket. "Listen, I wanted to ask you—"

"I'm engaged," I blurted.

Surprise covered his features, and then he furrowed his brow. "Oh." His eyes searched my face for understanding, so I held up my left hand.

"Yeah," I said. "Last month."

He nodded once. "Congratulations. That was—" He breathed in through his nostrils, and I knew the word he was going to say, but he politely stopped himself.

"Fast? Yeah, I know. But John knows what he wants, and it just... makes sense?"

"Is that a question?"

Yes.

"No, some things are just hard to explain, and the words are never right when you say them," I answered.

"Yeah, I know what you mean," he said. His lips twisted briefly, and then he patted the top of the box of books. "Well, thank you for these. Um, take care of yourself, okay?"

"Okay." My voice was small and unrecognizable even to my own ears. I was sure about John. He courted me. He set expectations, and I met them. I told him my dreams, and he made promises to fulfill them. We checked each other's boxes and crossed off each itemized part of a relationship until we were six months in, picking out wedding rings.

I fell in love with John.

So, it was painful for me to realize Isaac could unsettle me that quickly.

As he opened the door to exit, the chime rang, and the crisp, cold February air cut through the store, sending a breeze through my hair.

"Isaac," I called. He paused and turned. "What were you going to ask me?"

His eyes fell to the floor, then to the box of books he was holding, before returning back to me.

"Nothing that matters now," he said, a sad yet genuine

expression on his face. "Happy Valentine's Day. I hope your fiancé gives you the life you deserve."

fifteen

NOW

"Are you ready for the grand opening?" my sister, Jenn, asks as she dusts the shelves of the romance section.

"No," I admit, straightening bookmarks for the umpteenth time.

My sister, Marie, places a hand on mine. "I'm proud of you, Anna. I know walking away from John last year was hard, and you could have given up and felt sorry for yourself. Instead, you built this."

She gestures to the bookstore—warm wooden floors, original to the building, etched with scuff and life and memories. Floral wallpaper adorns the back wall, and endless rows of white shelves house all the trendy favorites and the classics—romance, thriller, true crime, historical fiction, and fantasy. Each book selected with purpose. Two separate

75

reading nooks have emerald green velvet couches and wooden end tables. The exposed brick wall houses a neon pink sign with the name of my bookstore hanging above the wine dispensaries.

Wine About Books.

This bookstore has always been my dream. Wine tastings and books. It pairs better than cheese, if you ask me.

I smile, soaking in the beauty of my own accomplishment. I did it. Finally.

The front door chimes open and I hear his voice. The voice of a stranger, yet so achingly familiar.

"I heard someone ordered some wine." His blue eyes are bright, and the smile lines around his eyes remind me of the years I missed out on him.

He makes me smile more than I ever thought I could. And maybe none of it makes sense. We didn't fall in love or have any time of longevity between the two of us when we met. But in thirty-six hours, we created a memory that couldn't be replaced, replicated, or forgotten.

After my divorce was finalized nine months ago, I focused on this dream project of mine. I carefully picked the new floor stain and sampled nearly thirty different kinds of wallpaper. I poured over book lists, deciding which would perfectly fit on these shelves. And when it came time to find the supplier for the wine, I knew exactly who to call.

One business call turned into coffee. Then dinner. Then, sunset picnics, trips to the city, and hikes in the mountains until each moment we spent together was strung together, and we realized the spark we felt all those years ago never died. It was just waiting for the right time for us to let it burn.

"Hey, stranger," I say, stepping to him, throwing my arms around his neck, and breathing him in.

"Are you excited?" he asks, sweeping a hand through my hair.

"Terrified," I answer.

He smiles. "Good. The best things in life should scare you a little bit at first."

I reach up on my tiptoes and kiss him on the lips.

Jenn claps twice. "All right, enough of that. We have work to do. Chop, chop. Isaac, can you bring in the cases of wine and put them in the back room? Marie and I will start loading the dispensary. Anna, can you polish wine glasses? We don't want your opening night to be destroyed by dust bunnies in wine."

"That would be a tragedy," Isaac agrees, albeit sarcastically.

Jenn glares at him. "Hey, we still like you. Don't screw up now."

We spend the next hour hustling, ensuring everything is in its perfect place. The spines of the books are perfectly lined up. The Wi-Fi password is hooked up. The cash register is on. The bathrooms are clean. And the bright red ribbon is tied together in a bow in front of the store, ready for me to slice through it with giant scissors.

"Take a moment and breathe it in before everyone arrives," Isaac says, handing me a glass of champagne. "I'll wait outside."

It is a cliché love story to myself. It's a Valentine's Day where I get to love the life I'm living. I take a lap around the store. I love it here.

The design and the concept.

The smell of the pages.

The labor of my love.

When I reach the front again, I step outside and clink glasses with Isaac. He is the bonus. The cherry on top. The second chance I never thought I'd get or even need.

He kisses me softly, then looks deep into my eyes. "What's next, Anna?"

I sigh into his embrace. "I guess it's time for you to meet my kids."

Mild concern flashes in his eyes, but he otherwise puts on his game face, tilting my chin to kiss me again. "I didn't think I'd ever get the chance to fall in love with you again."

My cheeks warm, and I feel flushed and hot. "You're

making me blush."

He swipes a gentle thumb over my cheekbone. "It's okay. Red is my favorite color."

acknowledgments

First, I want to thank my loyal readers for letting me be so chaotic. I have ideas and plans for the future at all times, but then, every so often I have an impulsive thought and decide to release something early or just because.

That's this story.

This is my why-not novella. My get-it-off-my-desk novella, if you will.

I also loved writing these characters, so thank you for accepting it with so much excitement. I would not be able to keep doing this without your support. Thank you, readers.

Alejandra Andrade, Trisha Harris, Abigail Ennis, Kelsey Kennedy, Riley Quezada, Jessica Williams, and Cristina Montero for being my early readers and falling in love with this story. I appreciate all of you so much for taking my early drafts and telling me whether or not this is a salvageable story. I love each of you.

Huge thank you to my editor, Jamie McGillan. You catch the sneakiest errors, and it allows me to breathe a sigh of relief after you've had your eyes on it.

And last, thanks to my family. I'm fully aware I work in thirty-minute bursts throughout the day and night so you never know if you're going to catch me in the middle of a scene or have my full attention. I love you all so dang much. Thank you for continuing to put up with me.

XO,
Caitlin.

about the author

Caitlin Moss is the author of eight books. She lives in the Pacific Northwest with her husband, three children, and two goldendoodles. She loves connecting with her readers on social media.

For more visit caitlinmossauthor.com.

caitlinmossauthor

caitlinmosswrites

caitlinmossauthor

CaitlinRMoss

Made in United States
Troutdale, OR
02/02/2024

17396122R00054